This book belongs to:

_Lois Bacher_

First published 2020 by Walker Books Ltd
87 Vauxhall Walk, London SE11 5HJ

This edition published 2021

2 4 6 8 10 9 7 5 3 1

© 1990–2021 Lucy Cousins
Lucy Cousins font © 1990–2021 Lucy Cousins

The author/illustrator has asserted her moral rights

Maisy™. Maisy is a trademark of Walker Books Ltd, London

Printed in China

British Library Cataloguing in Publication Data:
a catalogue record for this book is
available from the British Library.

ISBN 978-1-4063-9986-8

www.walker.co.uk

# Maisy's Chinese New Year

## Lucy Cousins

WALKER BOOKS
AND SUBSIDIARIES
LONDON • BOSTON • SYDNEY • AUCKLAND

Tomorrow is Chinese New Year.
Maisy sweeps and tidies
the house to get it ready!

Then, Maisy visits a market to buy food,
decorations and lovely new clothes.

Red is a lucky colour.
What red things can you see?

At home, Maisy waits for her first guest.

Who's that knocking at the door?

It's Tiger! She has come home to celebrate. Hooray!

Tallulah, Charley and Cyril arrive next.
"Welcome home, Tiger!" they all say.

Tiger has brought lots of presents and decorations to wish everyone happiness and luck.

They all sit at the table
to eat a delicious feast.
There are so many
things to try.

After dinner, Ostrich
and Penguin come to visit!
They give everyone lucky red
packets with money inside.

"Thank you!" says Maisy.

Maisy and her friends sit to listen to Tiger telling an exciting Chinese New Year story.

"A long, long time ago, twelve animals raced across a great river..." she begins.

"The rat won the race, but we celebrate every animal in turn.

dog

pig

rooster

monkey

goat

horse

rat

ox

tiger

rabbit

dragon

snake

And this makes up the twelve-year Chinese zodiac," Tiger explains.

The next day, everyone goes to a wonderful parade. It's so much fun!

Finally, Maisy leads her friends in a special dragon dance for good luck.

Happy New Year, Maisy! Happy New Year, everyone!

# Can you find?

sweet rice
cakes

dumplings

lantern

blossom

bamboo

mandarins

red packet